Z. A. Soliman is a 27-year-old graduate from dental school. She believes that a person can be more than one title. They can be a dentist, writer, artist, musician and even a professor. And to convince people of this, she decided to prove it to herself first. Writing is her salvation, the only place she can express freely. She is an Aries; once she sets a goal, she achieves it and won't be satisfied until her work, life and plans meet her dream life.

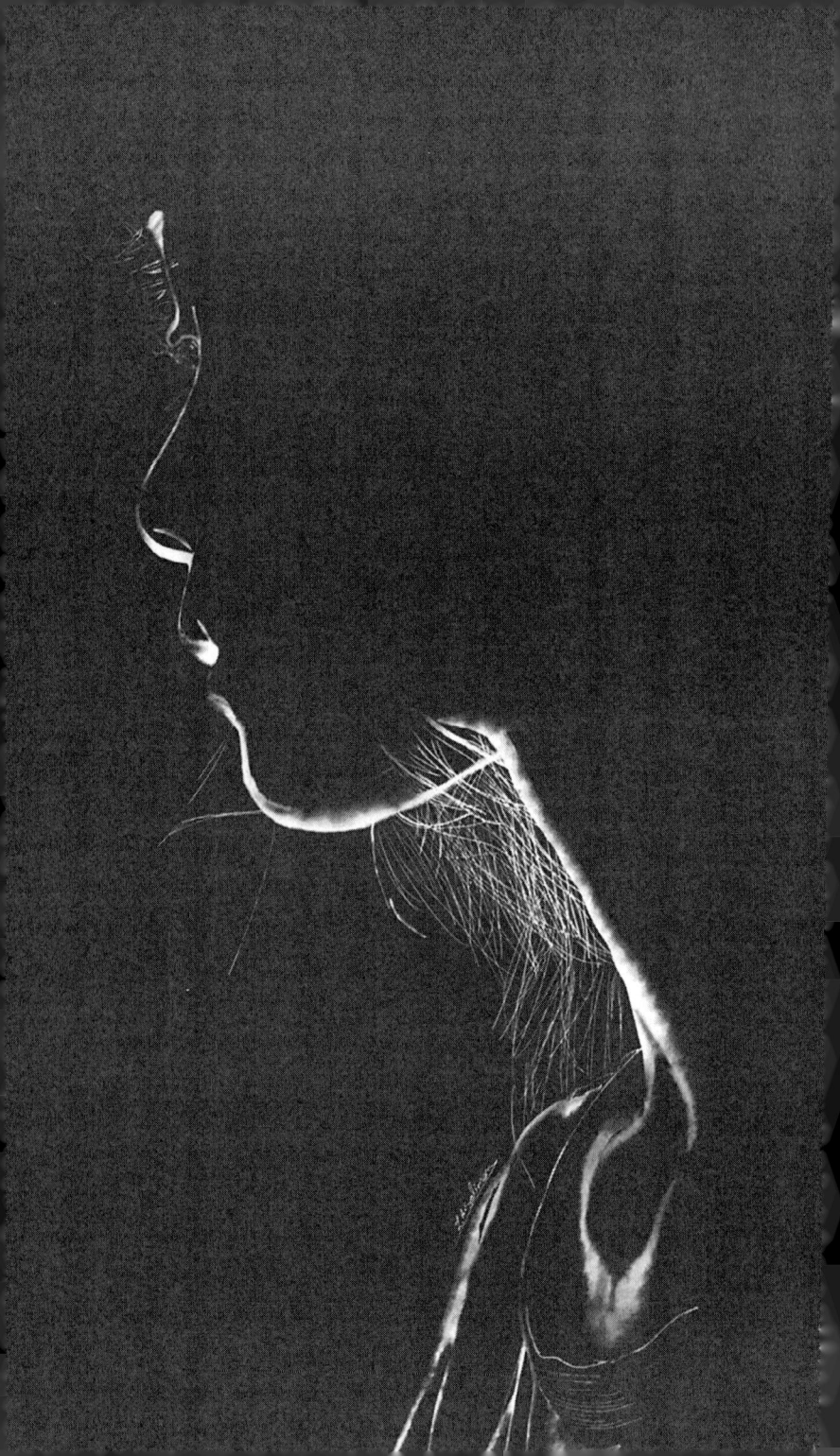

DIVINE Decree

The Truth Behind It

Z.A. Soliman

Austin Macauley Publishers™
LONDON · CAMBRIDGE · NEW YORK · SHARJAH

Copyright © Z.A. Soliman (2020)

The right of **Z.A. Soliman** to be identified as author of this work has been asserted by her in accordance with Federal Law No. (7) of UAE, Year 2002, Concerning Copyrights and Neighboring Rights.

All rights reserved. No part of this publication may be reproduced, stored in a retrieval system, or transmitted in any form or by any means, electronic, mechanical, photocopying, recording, or otherwise, without the prior permission of the publishers.

Any person who commits any unauthorized act in relation to this publication may be liable to legal prosecution and civil claims for damages.

The age group that matches the content of the books has been classified according to the age classification system issued by the National Media Council.

ISBN – 9789948347088 – (Paperback)
ISBN – 9789948347071 – (E-Book)

Age Classification: E
Application Number: MC-10-01-6112120

Printer Name: iPrint Global Ltd
Printer Address: Witchford, England

First Published (2020)
AUSTIN MACAULEY PUBLISHERS FZE
Sharjah Publishing City
P.O Box [519201]
Sharjah, UAE

www.austinmacauley.ae
+971 655 95 202

This book is nothing but thoughts of a reader, a lover and a deceiver. The words have been smoothly written from a passionate heart and soul of a dreamer, which could be real, real enough to believe in. It takes you to a different era, an imaginative world that you can simply relate with your own world. And because this world is very realistic—so dark, cold, and exhaustive—it needs some imagination to colour it, to feel the warmth of the sun and feel alive one more time. And so does he, he needs her light, her warmth and the purity within her. But with time you will realise that without darkness, the light wouldn't come; without reality, imagination wouldn't exist; and without him, she would never grow.

What has been said from the heart goes safely to the heart, settles down there and engraves deeply into it, forever. So go to your favourite corner with your favourite drink, dim the light, set your mind free and let your soul touch the words and feel what they felt.

Meanwhile, let my heart feel alive one more time.

The feelings I buried, the things I went through, the memories I carried about us. That specific memory that hit my heart out of nowhere, takes me to no place, lost. When I thought I forgot, when I thought I let it go, when I thought all these feelings are dead. When I thought I lost your image, but then I see you in all men.
Oh boy, there is a side in my heart you grew on and then buried it alive.

You will always be immortalised in my words.

"You are a good writer, and our love is a story that must be told, spread your ink over the papers and you will create a bestselling book," he said.

And so she did, she spread gasoline over the papers and watched her love story burn to ashes. I still can hear your voice whispering to my ears.

"You are a perfect writer, write about us. Our story is not like any other. Make it the first book of yours. Write what you couldn't tell." It takes all the courage and power in the world to write. Fear haunts my soul the moment I hold the pen because I remember things, things that I haven't forgotten but locked and buried deep in my heart. It took me seasons, it took all my strength, every teardrop and every breath to let it go and move on. Ever since this day I have not written a word, ever since that time I've lost my identity. Everything reminds me of you.

You're like a ghost that haunts me forever. The food, mostly desserts, reminds me of how much we were eagerly competing over who eats more. This dark coffee reminds me of your favourite café: Costa. I never liked Costa; my favourite was Starbucks. I can hear you saing, "Starbucks! It has nothing to do with the taste
of coffee, it's just a mix of flavour! Costa is the real
coffee maker." All the places remind me of you, even the ones we never went to. You're like a ghost that haunts me forever, living in my darkness. What will happen when I start to write and all these memories cross by? I know there will be sentences where my tears drop and chapters where I laugh out loud. But what about the words where my heart starts to call your name, my soul

searches for you and my dark side misses yours? Does your soul still remember mine? Does your heart recall mine? Does my name cross your mind when someone calls yours? Does your dark side meet mine secretly?

I can't tell where this will lead and how it will end, although those pages are numbered, I can't predict how much more it needs to end this chapter of my life.

I never thought about love and being loved in return. I believed that true love will find me wherever I am and it will widely open the door and settle down at the deepest point of my heart. And when it does, this love will be locked forever, secured. You, you said love is a beautiful thing to feel and that you have loved once. You loved her much and so did she, but at the end you both agreed to let it go, and ever since, you became more realistic and thought it is better to do things that matter most and love was the last thing to think about. But then our paths crossed…

Destiny

You have just walked out of my dreams to be real.

"Who is your dream girl?"
"Look at the mirror and you will see her,"
He whispered.

Unreachable, untouchable, like the universe you are.
Like the universe, you have my back.
Like the universe, you are my time, my energy, my every single detail.
Like the universe, I feel your breath through the wind, your happiness in spring and your warmth in winter.
Like the universe, you are indescribable.
I wonder how someone like you can overturn all the balances. Have you ever heard the morning birds tweet at night? Because that is your joyful voice.
Do you know that you are an aura of feelings moving?
You are similar to a basket of rose petals they use in wedding ceremonies, spreading joy and love.
You are a magnetic field that attracts hearts. But your sadness has no way to hide or is maybe trying to reserve a seat for you to learn happiness.
He is shy from his presence between us and how dare he appear in public under the influence of your aura. That cold night, I lay on my bed and shut my eyes, held my breath and focused in the darkness, listening to the movement within my soul.
I slowly noticed that the tick tock of the clock is no longer ticking and the sound of the wind is no longer wheezing. Somewhere in the dark, I could see the light, unclearly moving, getting closer to my sight. Then finally, everything was clear, everything made sense, I saw you and then the coldness of the room got conquered by warmth, the warmth of your breath. You are my universe.

There is chaos in your beauty Like the chaos of the stars And without this chaosThe sky wouldn't be glowing at night.

You are an old soul that can be slightly dramatic.
You express yourself through writing, music and art.
You can be friendly and open, yet closed and private.
Winter is your season.
When everything is cold and lifeless, the warmth of your breath is the guide to life.
Pure, like a diamond, your soul is.
In this dangerous world, you were born, fighting against the darkness of the storm.
Guard up, keeping your purity safe.

She was smart and wise by her own. Crazy for what she loves.
Owned a heart of angels, pure and crystal.
She wasn't perfect; her flaws were the best in her.
She could take anything she wanted with a smile.
That was how she had my heart in the first place.

"A smile like yours can make people die for it. Can I die now?" he said.
"Please don't, then I will not smile," she replied in rush.
"I adore this smile, please keep it; it illuminates spirits in hearts."
She smiled, blushing.
"Your smile is a heavenly thing, not from earth, I guess,"
he whispered.

She has a unique ability to see the best in people which allows her to stay positive and loved.
Her curiosity leads her to conventional wisdom. She is transparent and that makes them more curious about her.
She isn't a woman who takes "no" for an answer and that leads her to an adventurous life.

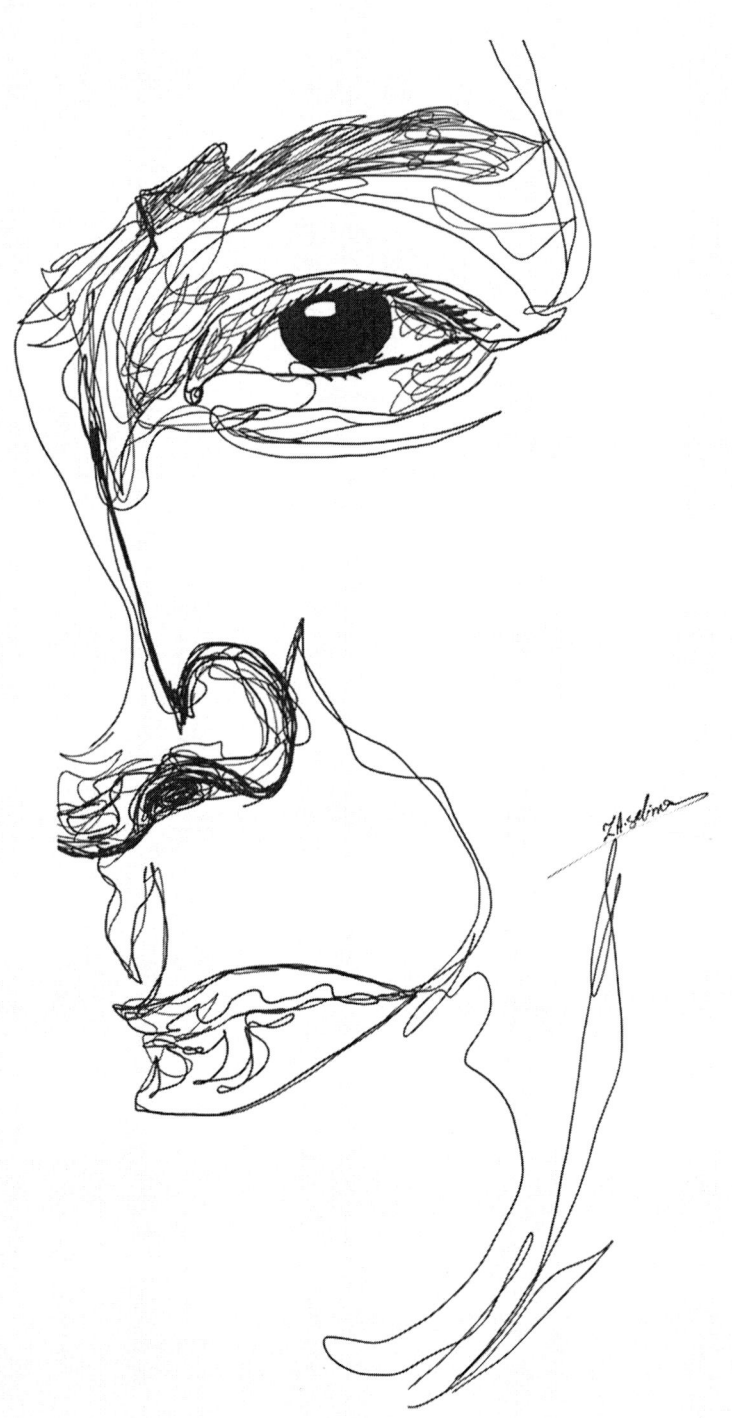

"I never felt alive like I did with you. I have a busy life. I am in a relationship with work and I thought this is where my happiness is, until I knew you; and ever since, I can't wait to wake up in the morning to text you. I no longer play music on the highway road; your voice is my enjoyment and during meetings, I grab my phone secretly to check on you.
You made me alive again and no woman ever did that."
I was so happy. I still remember and feel those feelings; it was indescribable, but I never thought of loving you.
Love was the last thing on my mind and being a friend was a great thing to have. But you had another plan or let me say, for now, destiny had another plan.
"Are you a writer?" a manly voice struck my thoughts. "May I ask what are you writing?"
Memories, I thought I forgot them, but it seems not.
"Love story?"
I'm quite not sure if it's just about love. You see, everything happens for a reason, and I don't believe these memories are just for love, there must be something bigger than love.
"Love is a big thing," he said in an intense voice.
"It is! But there are things bigger that make love last longer. Like honour, faith, forgiveness, knowledge, keeping promises and above all, choice."

I said the last word as I'm saying it to myself. This single word brought many memories back, memories I still strive to keep in the dark.
Again, his voice interrupted my own hidden world, "Did you say choice? What was yours?"
I looked up to where he was standing, "I'm sorry, can I order my drink after a while?"
I didn't wait for his mumbled response. Preferably, I looked back to my scattered writings, looking for empty lines to release these thoughts in and once I detected a blank space, my hands numbed, my thoughts dropped, my heart rate increased and my chest started to shrivel. My despair and the darkness within me aroused my sympathetic nervous system.
Lord, how I changed from being a girl whose words are her strengths, her hideaway, to being a girl who fears to write.
"Choice," I whispered. I must choose, either to live in fear or face it, deny the truth or accept it. Where are the blank papers? I flipped and scattered the papers again. Here is one. I took a deep breath then exhaled. I pounded my chest. "Everything will be alright," I said, listening to my heartbeats getting quieter and slower.
The heart that had been through much. The only part in my life that followed me in all my choices without complaining how much pain I was carrying, never leaving me alone through the journey.
I owe my heart much!

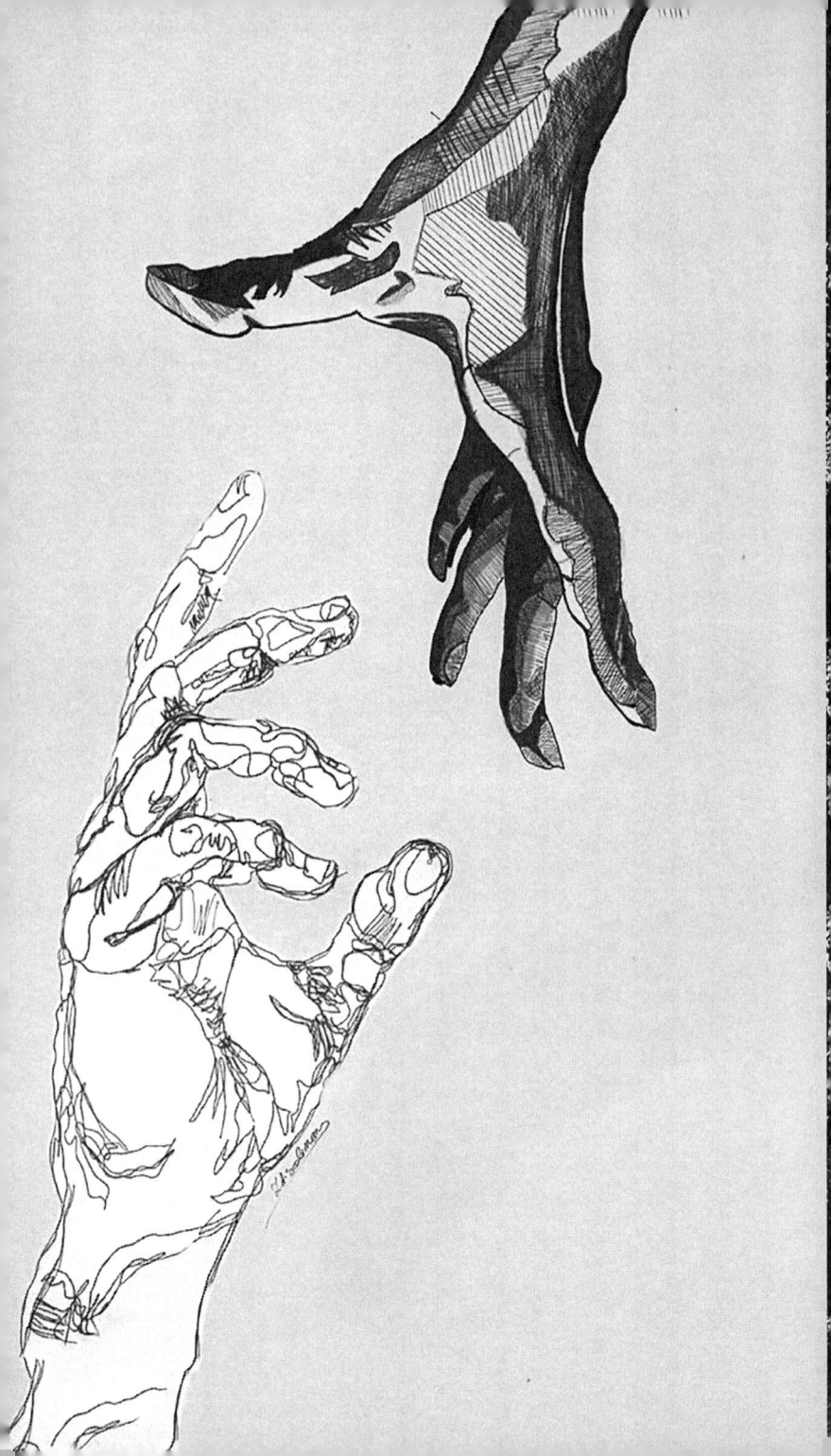

Choice

In another life I will still choose you.

Destiny is something divine you have no control of. But at a certain time of your life, it's not destiny; it's choice. Meeting you was destiny, but whatever comes after this day is a choice, and the power of choice is as much of a curse as it is a blessing. It is a double-edged weapon which can either take you to the right path or lead you into taking dreadful and regretful decisions. I know I will never regret choosing you, I trust my heart with this decision so before you go away, before destiny has another plan, stay in my world, and breathe my air because memories are the only thing we can have. So please let us create as many memories as we can.

She immersed deeply into the zenith of his heart, neglecting all the facts that he will never be hers.

She loved him with all his imperfections. She loved the darkness of his eyes and the darkness within him.

I know this road will lead to chaos, but this is how my love is. You are evil. You're very bad but I love you. I love you to darkness. In your heart I'm trapped and I can't find the light. But maybe struggling is what keeps us together. Maybe the way of seeing each other differently and believing in one another is what keeps us holding onto the dream even though it is hard to achieve.

Maybe this is meant to happen for a cause, for a reason. Although I can't see what is behind this, but aren't the feelings we feel enough?!

"I love your smile
Keep it on
It took me ages to see it!"
He said.

I found love
Love in a child's smile
Love in a mother's care
Love in an old man's wrinkles
Love in a friend's support
I found love in fights
Love in food
Love in tears
And love in letting go
And that love is what keeps me stronger
Everything makes sense until it comes to love
And you never made sense to me
But I loved you as if I was Newton
And you're the law of gravity.

"What do you want?"
She said with torment:
"Anything that keeps me in your heart,"
He answered with a smile.

At first I thought existing and asking for nothing is enough.
I was fully satisfied. Then I wanted more. I was addicted to a certain type of heroin. I was addicted to you.
The overdose of you wasn't enough. Then I thought I must quit but I was clueless about the symptoms.
Every cell in my body started to burn. My heart began to collapse and I felt the urge for the drug.
The urge for you, because simply once, I heard your voice
And I knew
This is the sound I want to wake up with
Every morning for the rest of my life

"Love is written on your face
You believe in what you found
I'll be lost in time and space
Until I hear that sound
I want to hear you say it
Doesn't get any better than this
If this ain't really love
Then tell me baby what it is?
Without you I can't breathe
What do you promise me?
I want to hear you say it
I want to hear you say it"
Michael Bolton—I WANNA HEAR YOU SAY IT.

Remember our first date? It was like hide-and-seek. I woke up early that day and I thought, Let us have lunch together, and when I told you, you couldn't believe it.
"Finally, you said yes!"
But then you had a meeting that would finish at four and I had to catch up a meeting at five.
We only have one hour or maybe less. I felt down and because I didn't eat the whole day, I was hungry too.
"One hour is better than never, right? Let me invite you to a restaurant you never went to before."
"What restaurant?" I asked.
"It is a surprise; you will know when we get there. Now get ready, at 4 sharp I will pick you up."
I was so excited, my friend was also excited, "Finally, you will get the chance to meet your mysterious guy. I pray you fall in love with him!" she said.

I was! But I didn't say it to anyone.
I was deeply in love, and it was the greatest feeling ever.
It takes you so high up to heaven, the attraction of love pulls you to the centre of the universe.
I loved you and I fell too deep in the apex of your heart.
And I want you to hear it, today.

As you said, at 4 pm you were in my place.

I walked out of the door and once I was near to your car, the car door opened and out emerged a tall, broad-shouldered man who had his black army-style shades to protect his eyes from the striking sun. He was wearing classic navy pants, the classic shoes of the same colour and a chaotic light blue shirt, finishing his outfit with a white dotted sky blue tie and a silver tie clip. I kept walking, trying to stop my feet, but my body suddenly became someone else's and I no longer had the power to control it, as if all the gravity of the earth was from you and you were pulling me to you.

We were so close. I've never been close to a man like that before. The aura around you was so charming and secure.

I had to exert a force on my feet to stop and to resist your gravity; I had to stop at a certain point. You smiled and said with your joyful voice, "Hi. Ready?" I nodded and got into the car.

I was terrified, not from you, I was terrified from my braveness.

What was I doing? I never got into a man's car before! I was saving this memory for my future husband.

You looked at me and saw my fear. You calmed me down, you didn't move the car till I told you to and when I did, you looked at me again and said, "Seat belts, please."

Gosh, I laughed that day. I kept saying it all day, mimicking your voice, "Seat belts, please."

You were getting out of the parking when suddenly, a humming bird showed up crossing the street and, surprisingly, you stopped.
You let the bird cross safely and with no rush.

I looked at you and thought…
Your heart will keep me safe because somewhere in your heart there is a small light and there is where I will live.
"YES!" you shouted and I freaked out. I looked at you. "Are you crazy? What's wrong with you?"
"Finally, you're here. Today is my best day and all the days you're with me will be my best days."
My face turned red and then I remembered how hungry I am and I needed to eat right then. So I asked you where we are going.

"Since we have less than an hour, our restaurant will be here in the car, I'm sure you've never been in such a place," you said with your joyful voice.
"No, not in your car," I mocked.

We stopped in front of the subway, you asked me to come with you to order but I preferred to stay in the car. I couldn't feel my legs. I was still surprised at what I was doing, but I wasn't scared, actually I never felt safe as I did that time.
While we were waiting for our drink and before we ate, I studied the details of your face: the jaw line, the smooth, slight, black beard that gives you a masculine look, and the white fine hair showing in your dark hairs toward the side. It was those black eyes that I couldn't stop looking at.
I studied your face as if it will be the last time I will see you, memorising your figure, breathing deeply to intake as much of your perfume as I can, as if I'm filling my lungs with it.
You infringed this silence with three words.

"I love you."

4:55 pm, five minutes left for my meeting. I was late but I didn't care, even if being late will put me in trouble and lead to all sorts of questions. As long as I'm with you, I'm safe.

"No, I will not put the girl I love in a difficult situation. If 5 pm you should be there, then you will." I admired that. I felt like a princess that time. "Seat belts, please."

I giggled and put the belt on. We reached my place on time; the vehicle that was supposed to take me to the meeting was driving on the opposite road. You pressed the horn, slid the window down and asked the driver to wait.
You looked at me and said, "I'm assured now that you're the right girl, thank you for showing up in my life."
The driver pressed the horn from his bus in order to hurry me up.

I released the seat belts, opened the car door and got off the car. I turned on my back, partially closed the door then turned back to you, opened the door wide and said,
"I love you too."

Truth

Sometimes the best thing in your life is borrowed.
That is why it goes back to its owner.

This is a story of two souls who once became one.
With all the difficulties and nature of earth, they were able to survive everything for the name of love.
Although coincidence made that happen, destiny had a different plan.
They were warriors, warriors fighting with weapons of love and peace.
But who can win a battle against destiny?
Pens have been lifted and pages have dried.
She felt weak and lost.
Sometimes even heroes need to fall to gain strength.
She ran and kept running, until she found herself in this pure place, calm and safe.
She went through with no hesitation and fell down the floor like a dead leaf in autumn season falling from the old tree.
She prayed, yes, she spoke out loud.
"Lord, if he is good for me, keep him in my life and if he isn't good for me, you are capable of everything, make him good."
Oh yes, she couldn't accept the fact that he will never be hers.
It is ironic how even after you let go of something,
You still want it and desire it.
She didn't know how this would end. She didn't want it to end neither to have him end it.
Because for her, everything will begin to hurt and collapse once she let him go.

It is difficult to move on when you're still deeply engraved in my heart.
If I take you out of it, it will leave a gap.
And no one can fill this gap but you.

I sat alone
And thought to myself
Who would we be?
What would become of us?
If we meet in another world
At another time
In a different way
With different us
What if…

She knew he will not stay forever,
But she loved him as if he belonged to her.
She knew that her momentary happiness will become her tears for ages,
But she chose to dance at the edge of fire, rather than sleep in a golden room like a corpse.

I know you're not alone
And I'm not the only one
Who loved you.
But I'm the only one
Who lived in your heart.
The only one who touched your soul.
I know because there is no explanation for it.
I believe because I have not seen it.
But my soul, my mind, my heart and every cell in my body sensed you.

All those who I cared about were gone, either they left this life or left my life. They promised not to walk away and leave me alone. All who I loved waived from their promises. I didn't leave anyone, they did, and they completed the mission of life, the meaning of it, of mortality.

Nothing stays forever.
But in one way or another, if they were still alive, they'd end up appearing in front of my life's door, apologising and asking for forgiveness. It is only a matter of time.

And so I feared to love you and care about you, for you may also leave, and I neither wanted to lose you nor see you coming back, asking for forgiveness. Your rank in my heart is too high to ask for forgiveness.

Nevertheless, you promised and assured me that you're not like the others.
"I will not leave until you ask me to."
And I will never ask you to leave, how can I ask my heart to abandon its shelter, my body?

You were so sure of not leaving me or that's how you sounded. Your voice, that shivery voice, when you talked to me wasn't weakness, neither fear. It was love, the power of desire, the sound of passion, the force of darkness and you fear, it will conquer my light.

Through your life, everything you touched or loved died. The darkness within you murdered it, and my light, the pureness within me, made you forget your past and lightened up your

heart, but not until one night, when this passion woke up the beast in you, the king of all darkness.
You wanted to flee, leave me in peace and not to kill my innocence with your venom. I didn't understand this, I thought you were not sure about our relationship and I thought you feared to love again.

I held you; I gave you time to decide but no matter what your decision will be, I will not let you go. I loved you and who touches my heart will stay in it forever. I had to comfort your heart that it will be safe, safe with me.

I rested my hand on your chest and asked you a simple question. "What does your heart say?"

Passion

The Beauty and the Beast

She is a woman.
She has the ability to say "no" and "yes"; "I can" and "I can't."
She has the power of choice. She is a woman. She enjoys reading a book in a cafe and drinking hot chocolate under the rain. She is a woman that you can make her the happiest on earth with your simplicity.
She is a woman.
Speaks up with what she believes in out loud and there is no power on earth that can stop that from happening.
She is a woman with no mask.

But he was doomed by darkness when he sold his soul to demons of desires.
She knew from this moment that she will take a decision by her own.
The fear of losing him and the love that conquered her made her realise that everyone has a second chance and this is his.

There is no scale for a perfect life. It is how you see it and want it. She had everything in her hands yet she always felt like her hands were empty. She needed one thing, his imperfections. Because for her, this was her perfect life.

………

"Give it a chance
A chance to bring the good in you."
She believes, she does believe that deep in him lies a good heart.
"Give me a chance
Not to lose the good in me.
Don't let what's between us go with the wind"

She thinks.
"If I'm not having you, then let me leave you with good.
Let this destiny turn to be a good one.
Give it a chance
To know and love the best in me before it goes away.
Give it a chance to be your pureness, not your sin!"
She said

"That love that takes you to the darkest place, it takes me to the brightest place. It guides me to the purest land, your heart and your soul. Sometimes, and with the way you speak, I fall in love, in love with your words, in love with that passion and that strength. You give me shivers with your smile.
You make me fall in love with your purity. However, I'm afraid one day I will take away your purity.
Fulfil you with my darkness.
I fear one day you'll disappear within my shadow.
By then I will lose you and lose myself.
I've found heaven in your brown eyes.
What if you were doomed because of me?"

She interrupted his speech and asked him,

"What if my purity conquered your darkness?
And you were able to live in my heaven?
I know you will keep me safe.
I know because your fear will protect me…"
She assured him.

The truth is that his love was taking her to a dark place, while her love was taking him to a light place.
To be together, one of them had to go with the other.
It is always the dark that wins.

*He would say anything just to make her feel better.
Even if his words made no sense at all.
But he never failed to cheer her up.
And this was the beauty of love.*

I have always wanted to live in this era.
The time when waiting is full of passion, when you know that a late reply is not due to rejection but due to distance.
That when you read it, you actually hear it.
It's when you never stop reading it over and over again.
It's where a memory is kept alive.
It's when you grow old, you open that old box and all your love letters fall to the floor.
By then a drop of tear falls off.
While all your memories cross over your mind and you never ever lose that feeling.

She knew because she saw it
Deep through his dark eyes
He loved her in his own way
And he kept her safe
Safe from the demons
Because he to them
Was the king of darkness.

"You are an example of perfection,"

He said
"No one is perfect,"
She said, disagreeing with him
"To me you are,"
He whispered.

*"When you go fishing
You throw the bait and wait for the fish
Wait and wait
Longingly
So whenever I'm waiting
I call it fishing,"
He said.
"Have you ever waited but never caught a fish?"
She asked
"I don't remember,"
He said.*

Someone once said,
"When life thinks of kicking your back
Take a big turn and kick its."

What does a lost soul need more than a pure land?
A land to feel at home.
Safe and loved.
She was his pure land.
His heart
His home
And the only good in him.
She believed in him
Believed that behind a beast
Lay a good heart.
Otherwise, what will guide the beast to the beauty?

I'm your light
I'll guide you to the right path
I'm your bright side
That was buried for so long
I'm you
The good in you
I was born from your darkness
To light up your heart
I'm here now
You're no longer lost
And I will not allow the darkness to find you again

"Thank you for existing in my life."
"Don't thank me, thank the good times we had together."
"They wouldn't be good without you, it is you who made this come real."

"I will never forget you
I will always renew my memories with you
It is the only thing I want to keep alive
You are every cell in my body
You are my heart,"
He said.

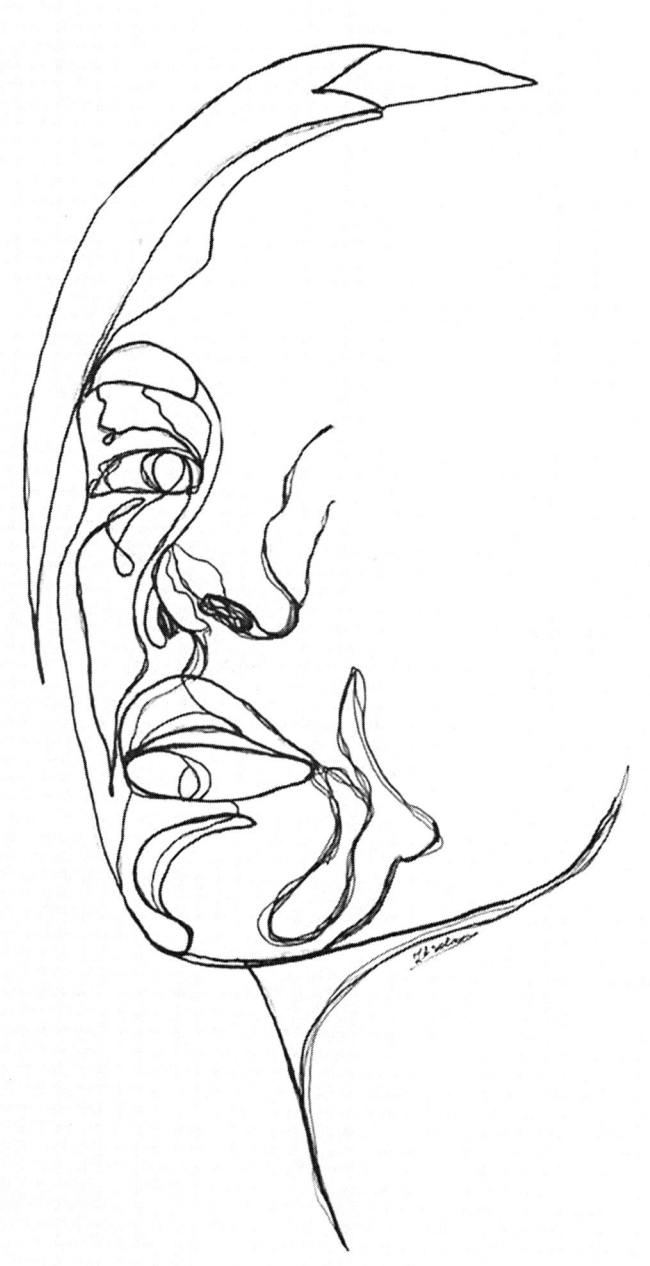

An old friend who recently broke up with her boyfriend asked me a simple question that was to her an important one. And before she asked me, she made me promise her to speak the truth and I promised.

***

"Am I beautiful? Don't mention my personality, I mean my figure, my body. Am I beautiful? What was wrong in me that made him leave me for another girl? I was so good to him. I must admit she has a perfect body." I thought a bit about what she said and how he made her think. She neglected the beauty of personality and had concerns about her figure.

***

Maybe this is the reason you were too good to him. Men like him want a woman to run after him, to make her suffer. Maybe the reason is because you're so beautiful in and out and this is too much for him.
Maybe because you are more than just a figure and he is nothing but an empty mind and that made him fear you.

***

I once asked the same question from you. "What is wrong with me, am I not enough for you?"
"Nothing is wrong with you, you are perfect the way you are, and stay that way. The mistake is not in you, the mistake is in me."

***

Before you, I had doubts, doubts in beauty. I'm not beautiful, my voice sounds deep. I hated hearing my voice in a video or on record. I disliked my figure and the colour of my skin. I never noticed how beautiful my smile is. I knew I had a good personality, but no man will notice that until he speaks to me and no man will approach to do so unless I'm beautiful and attractive from outside, or so I thought.

***

You came and you made me love the details of my hand, the tone of my voice, even my flaws. You loved every single detail in me, including my inner beauty. From that moment I had confidence; I now walk in a crowded room with confidence. When a man approaches and says I'm beautiful, I reply, "I am indeed beautiful and smart. There is more to me than what the eyes can see."
Outer beauty wasn't enough, I must tell others that I'm beautiful inside too.

***

My dear women, don't blame yourself for the collapse of a relationship. Don't underestimate yourself. You are perfect the way you are; love yourself, love your flaws and love your figure.

***

If a man wants you for your figure, this figure will not last long, we grow in age and all the beauty fades away at a certain time and this is life's norm. But your inner beauty will last forever.

***

Take a man who develops your inner beauty, who seeds confidence in you, who believes in you and respects you. Take a man who doesn't let you question yourself.

***

Don't wait for someone to say how beautiful you are. Say it to yourself, "I'm beautiful," because you truly are, you're beautiful just the way you are.

***

The truth is…your other half will appear when you understand who you are, what you want, what you desire and what you are missing, so that you can choose your partner right, knowing that person is the one to complete you.
The truth is most relationships fail because you don't know

what you want, you don't understand who you are, so you strike everywhere, creating chaos and dragging the poor fellow with you.
The truth is…you don't need someone to guide you to the right path or fix you, because no one knows you better than you.
The truth is…you know the truth and you choose to live in denial, fear of losing your comfort zone, fear of the unknown.

***

I don't know why and how, but I know I love you. And I know you love me too, although everything you do shows the opposite but I know somewhere deep inside, you love me.

***

The fact is that I'm good at showing it and you're good at hiding it We're completely different in everything and maybe these differences are what keep us holding on to each other so tightly. I live my life according to my heart's desire and you live your life according to your mind's soul.

***

Everything happens for a reason, right?
Maybe, maybe, your reason is to see the passion and sparkling light of life through my eyes.
While my reason is to know the reality of life through your soul before I hit the wall and to understand who I am and what I'm capable of.
Whatever the reason is, it brought us here together and as long as we are together, I shall not care about the reason.

Survival

As long we are together, we will surpass everything.

The deformity of being a highly imaginative person is that the mind never goes in sleep mode and the person ends up either extremely happy or desperate.
And whatever the result is, it never is compatible with reality. Imaginative minds never believe in realistic minds. Yet, they became one soul.

*I'm not safe without you
I'm safe with you
Your heart keeps me safe
Safe from myself.*

It's true that we meet people for reasons
Maybe his reason is to be like her
Because she never saw such a mind
Realistic and logical. She calls him "king of darkness"
because he never involves feelings while taking decisions
under any circumstances
Except one, and that decision was her.

*Stealing is a crime that must be punishable
And your sentence for stealing my heart
Shall be imprisonment in the deepest part of it.*

His morning texts are like the rising sun
Overcoming the darkness of the night
And her response is always like a bird
Singing and dancing in joy
The world understands nothing but a charming bird tweeting
Claiming the arrival of the morning
But the truth is…
The sun and bird are in love
And they announce it to the
World every morning.

"Why me?!"
She exclaims.
"Sometimes things happen with unknown reasons.
Reasons that you might not know now but you will later.
In fact, what drives me crazy here is that I have no answer for your question.
Why you? And why now? How could such a woman overturn all my balances?
But isn't it enough that only with you,
I feel all these feelings?
And when you are between my arms,
Our heartbeats unite,"
He whispers…

"Haven't you realised yet?!
We fought against it
We fought against our will
We walked away many times
But we still ended up together
Strongly connected
Like never before
Haven't you realised yet?!
It is our destiny.
And the day I'm letting you go,
Is the day when I will know you don't care about me anymore
It is the day I will not see your eyes sparkling for me,"
She said.
"That day will never come,"
He whispered.

Don't allow what brings us together to be the same reason that pushes us away.
I know you will keep me safe.
Safe in your heart.
I know because the details of your eyes say so.
The love and passion you carry for me.
Will keep me safe.
Safe from the rest of the world.

Friends?

—Lovers forever

They say, "You don't give the forehead kiss to anyone" and I wonder why. Is it because we grew witnessing our father giving it to our mother? Or a son kissing his mother's forehead as a meaning of "God bless you?" What does a forehead kiss mean? So I expanded my research and I found this;

Forehead kiss means gratitude. A silent word of "I care about you." In some societies it means apology, in others it means respect and friendship. It has many connotations but they all agree on one meaning; sincerity.
But let me tell you what it means according to how I sensed it. What feelings I had when his warm lips kissed my forehead. Remember? Remember this day? The day that I was forced to make a choice, and what choice is that when I'm obliged to choose. A choice of leaving you now or leaving you later! Does that even make any sense?!
Remember when I looked at your eyes to tell you good-bye forever, the word that I practiced saying many times, it was a drastic moment to say it and I couldn't. Instead I shrieked, I begged you not to make me choose, I buried my head into your chest and I yelled, telling you I can't let you go, don't go!

Remember what you did? You hugged me tight and kissed my forehead!
Silence overtook me for a moment.
That kiss is still engraved in my soul. In that moment you said things in silence. You said, "You are safe, my love." You assured me that you won't let that choice be hard for me. You told me without saying it how sorry you were. The amount of guilt you felt for making me reach this stage.

The stage where you promised me it won't happen. I felt your weakness, a strong man like you failed to take away the pain that he generated. He created it but didn't mean it and this was the part you apologized for without saying it. I felt love, I sensed pain, your pain. I felt affection and admiration. I felt you. And I couldn't comfort you, I couldn't take away the reality, our reality. We both were broken. But we both were in love!

Our reality is so beautiful and so painful. And for this I tend to go to my peaceful place, my imaginary world.
Note this, we sleep to dream of the things we can't achieve or feel in reality. We dream in order to escape from the painful truth, to create our own world, the life we've been dreaming of.

***

But sometimes we can't control our dreams, especially dreams that come from the unconscious mind.
Dreams come to us in many forms. If you are controlled by fear in reality, the fear of losing, the fear to be unloved, the fear of death, your dreams will come in the form of nightmares, darkness and anxiety! But if you're controlled by happiness, love and courage in reality, your dreams will come in forms of colourful butterflies, rainbow and sparkling light.

Sometimes dreams come in the form of denial of reality, a self-mechanism or you can say a human behaviour where a person chooses to deny reality as a way to avoid traumatic, uncomfortable facts and replace it by daydreaming. This type of dream is well-controlled but too much of anything is good for nothing.

At a certain point, you need to accept the reality and deal with it. Escaping and denial are not the right actions

***

Other times, when you escape from reality and sleep, you escape from the rejection of people around you or avoid stressful situations to find yourself in your dreams.

***

Whatever the case may be, your dreams are the reflection of who you are. So surround yourself with people who support and accept you for who you are, who help you to be creative in your reality and in your dreams.

***

But my case is different. I admire my reality, the existence of you in my world. Why would I dream when I have you in my world?

***

But as I said, sometimes your presence fades away and my soul fades along with you and my only salvation is my dreams, so I sleep in order to have you back, I sleep to dream of the world where you exist. But I can't control my dreams because of the fear of losing you, so I need you to embrace me with your light and shield me from the darkness of demons. Keep your innocence around me as an aura so that darkness shall not find me and fill my dreams with love and light. I need you to be in both my reality and my dreams.

Dreamer

If time is the thief of the day, then dreams are the place to stay.

She doesn't need a picture to remember him with.
She sees him in people's faces, hears his laugh in her laughs.
And his voice is deeply engraved in her memories.
She doesn't need anything to remind her of him.
He is unforgettable.

Hello there,
If you want to feel strong, be it at a moment of tribulation,
Stand up in front of a mirror, have a look at your reflection.
Close your eyes and have a quick flashback of your past.
The mistakes you did, the problems you had, the times you felt it was over; you can't take it anymore.
The feeling of weakness and the nonsensical words you said.
Open your eyes, who are you now? What have you become?
You're still standing out there, still smiling and still fighting for what you believe in.
You can feel the race of your heartbeats, still alive, still breathing!
Take every beat, every breath and every step to do what you want to do; it is the grace your Lord gave you.
A sign of "be better," don't waste that… Opportunity.

People believe because they have no reason not to, because they have proof.
They see it and touch it.
And I believe because the heart wants to.
Because the heartbeats whisper to my soul "believe."

"You look peaceful while you're sleeping," she said.
"Not really, I always run or climb a mountain or swim hard in my dreams
So I'm always intense while sleeping," he said.
"Just don't overdo in real life and you will find peace in your dreams," she whispered.

Stop running away. Don't shut yourself inside.
Open the door. Remove the fear from your heart and destroy the wall you built.
Face the places you fear and feel the pain.
Feel it till you no longer feel.
And then fill your heart with love and feel it.
Forever. You live once.
Try, fall, then get up and try again.
And have knowledge of everything and never fear to speak what's in your heart.
Feel all the feelings and then bury the negative ones, let only the positive thoughts overwhelm you.
Pray, laugh, love and run for your dreams.
Do what you always wanted to do, even if it is wrong.
Learn from your mistakes and then keep moving on.

Don't build dreams under a weak base.
It will fall.
All your hard work,
All your dreams will collapse.
And he had the weakest base,
Yet she couldn't stop dreaming.

Can I envy people with lost memories?
Because some memories are just too painful to remember
Or shall I feel sympathy for them because they have no past?
Do those who care about them have the right to keep some
past hidden in the dark, believing it is better to be forgotten?
And how can they trust them with some old photos and stories?

And when her loved one left the world
The darkness went to heaven
Where peace and light belong
She felt weak and fragile
But she had no time to grieve
She thought,
"The living are more important than the dead."

Wait, don't leave now. Stay, my soul hasn't let go of your soul.
My heart's still listening to the music of your heartbeats.
Wait, before you go. Leave a piece of you with me.
Like a tie clip.
So I can feel your shadow everywhere I go.
Or words from your voice.
To help me sleep at night with peace.
Or a stolen kiss.
To remind me of your passion.
Please, stay a bit more before you leave. It might be our last goodbye.

You know what is the worst feeling?
Holding on to something that leads nowhere,
Knowing that there is no hope!

She can't understand how she still feels safe with him after all his lies.
How she still believes his words when her mind says he lies.
Somehow his lies are keeping her safe.
Safe from the fact that he will never…
be her man.

There was a little boy who said, "I will run away when I can."
But there was a man who crossed my life.
And I thought the boy is right.
I will run away.
But not far from you.
I will run to you.
Because if you see what I saw,
If you feel what I felt and if you will seek as I seek,
Then you will run,
To me too.

"You know what's the best thing about nightmares? It's just a dream," he said.

Days proved to me that no one keeps secrets, their deepest, darkest secrets.
It's just a matter of time and a little trust with good communication until they open up their hearts to you and reveal their secrets as an open book.
Years taught me that everyone's struggling in life.
Whether with family, love, loss, money, education and worst, struggling with themselves. Yet, they always show their hardcore side.
Life showed me that it is a script and we are the cast and each one of us has multiple roles. And the truthful version of us, the real identity of us, is the time when we are all alone, when no one is watching and at this particular moment, it is the best version of us. I'm a lot! There is me with my teachers, me with my friends, me with my family, me with strangers and me with my love. Then comes the time when I'm alone and there I can be anyone at any time and no one can stop or judge me and that is my truthful version of me.
So when you come and judge me, which version of me are you judging? In fact, how can you be sure that I showed you the right one? Maybe, and just maybe, I'm manipulating your mind, wanting you to judge me the way I want.

***

I'm lonely and lost. There is nothing left for people to take when they leave for I've been already left with nothing but emptiness. But none of them broke me, none of them led me to insanity and devastation.
I'm still holding on, still have one last piece intact, the piece that brings me up when I collapse.

And I fear you'll take the last piece left, my mind. I fear when I let you in, you will fulfil my emptiness with love and happiness. I fear when you do that, I will forget who I was before and forget how to get up when life hits me hard.

And most of all, I fear when you leave, you will take it all away along with my last piece, my mind, and leave me alone on the ground, lost, no idea how to get up and how to face life all alone.

Love fulfils the void in your body. Removes the insecurities you have. Answers the questions you asked from yourself. Am I pretty? Am I enough? Am I worth it? Am I smart? 'Who am I?

Love fills all the emptiness in your body and makes you complete. This is when you know love is real. But when love goes away, the body remembers.

It remembers all the voids, all the emptiness and all the insecurities. It remembers the harsh words and the dark nights. The body remembers even after the mind forgets. The reasons why Alzheimer's people get to be reminded of their past with photos, a slow dance, a familiar voice, a known touch is because the body remembers.

And my body will remember you. Your love will fulfil all my emptiness and answer all my questions. So when you leave, my body will remember all the questions and all the doubts will return in a bigger form. And it will be so hard to fulfil it again, so hard to trust love again. You are not only taking memories away, you are taking my soul along with you, and I fear this!

For now I've got nothing to give and nothing to lose. For now I'm empty.

So stay where you are, I don't need to be saved by a hero, I don't need new promises to be broken, I don't need love. I don't want my body to know there is something as sweet in life as love. "I will never leave you, unless you ask me to do so. I promise I will never break your heart nor break you down. Give me the chance to show you what life truly is. You don't need a hero, you only need to let me in," he said.

"I fear that I will never ask you to leave. I fear I will be too weak and accept the least of what I deserve instead of letting you go. I fear I will love you more than myself and my weakness will be you.

I fear you will keep hurting me but my love will blind me from

the truth, the truth that I was right. I fear the day your sparkly eyes will fade away when you look at me and realise you're no longer in love with me.

I fear that my first regret ever will be letting you in," she said.

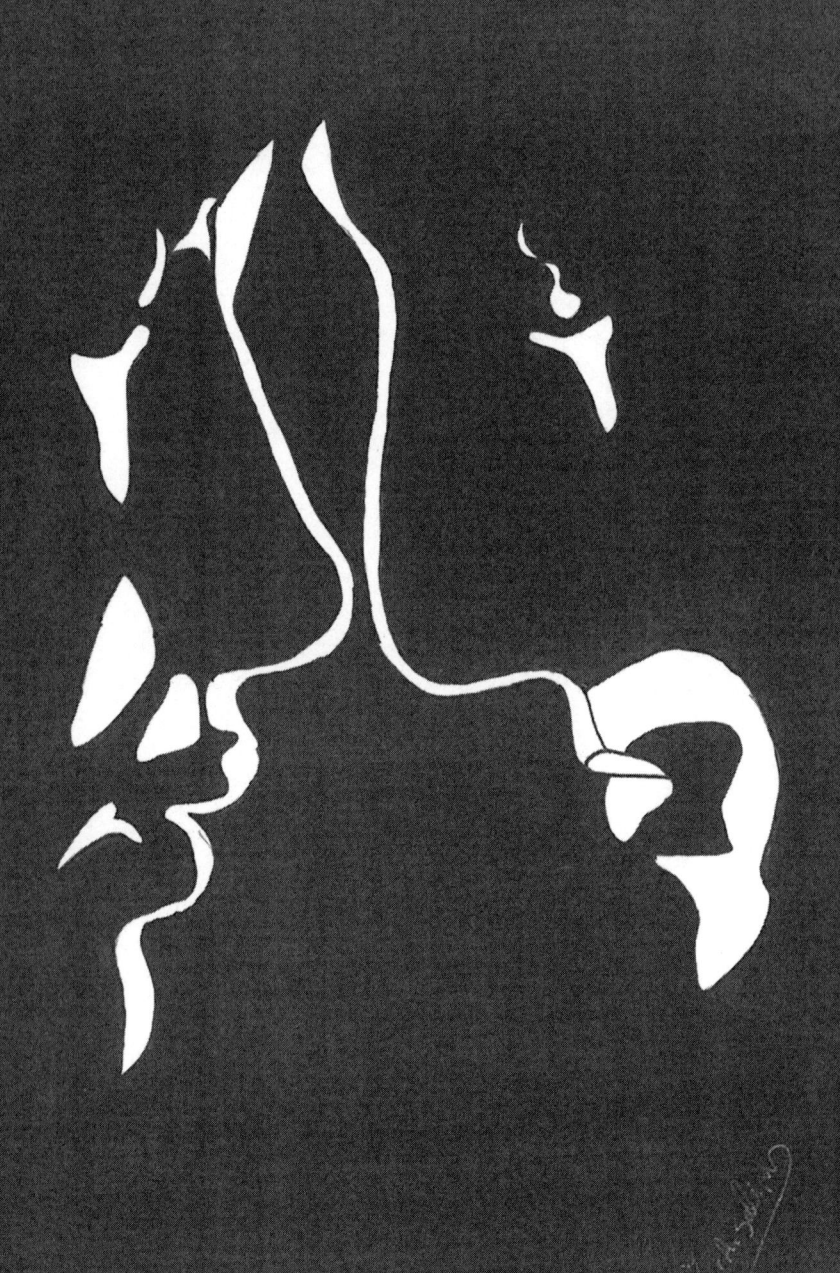

Fear

The fear of losing is what makes you lose.
Control your fear or fear will control you.

Thantophobia
(n.) the fear of losing someone you love.
Her irrational actions are for reasons.
Strong, reasonable reasons.
She fears losing him.
She fears one day she will wake up and realise he is gone.
She still hasn't had enough of him.
She still has much to give, much to tell and much to do.
So, she is taking every chance to be with him.
Every second to say how much she loves him.
She is not done yet, no, she is not.

And when you own happiness
Fear comes over
Reminding you of the chance of losing it!
So shall we allow fear to come between us
And destroy the happy moments?
Or we defeat fear
That is only created by us
And overcome it with happiness?
It is all in our hands.

*Don't end any conversation with a "goodbye"
It feels like it is your last goodbye.
And because my soul is still in you,
I fear the day I lose myself.*

It is a feeling that happens once in a lifetime.
You can't just let it go.
There is no weakness in being unable to forget what matters to you most.
What touched your soul can never be forgotten.
And whoever says, "Everything ends sooner or later," hasn't felt what you felt.
You got to take risk at a certain point, and when you do, never regret.
You had made your choice, now it is time to guide it to the right path.

*And when the cage was opened
She couldn't set her wings free
She was too fragile to fly high
Too old to feel alive again
Fear finally found its way to her
Pure soul.*

I can't say goodbye
When I'm not sure it is the final goodbye
Because I'm tired
I'm tired from leaving and coming back
And you'll always be there
Waiting for me
I can't reach my final decision
It is difficult
And I thought
I thought I'm capable of
anything
But not this, not you.
I need the man who loved me back.
He was sweet, lovely, funny.
And thirsty for me.
He wanted to know more about me.
Excited for anything related to me.
Loved how silly I could be,
How I acted dumb sometimes.
That man had a special look for me,
No one else had seen it before.
But I can see now how I'm losing you.
It kills to lose you when you still exist.

*"Slowly desire fills the room
Slowly I feel my soul consumed
I'm losing myself in you…"*
Michael Bolton—SLOWLY

A gift from heaven is unique, it is a blessing but it can sometimes be a scourge if it's only used against nature of life. What if you can predict your future, your times of success and failures, your moments of happiness and sadness?

What if you can see your death, would this still be a blessed gift from the unlimited sky?

I met a palm reader, a friend of mine who revealed her biggest secret of knowing a person's life just by looking at his or her palm. Those curvy, rigid, smooth, unpatterned lines are your future. Would you want to know? Will your curiosity take over you?

We were in her favourite cafe, her second home, catching up to the day's events, when she suddenly held my hand and turned it around to face my palm to her hazel eyes.

"You know how to read palms?" I asked with doubt.
"You know, I don't know how, but yes I do, I never read about it but I have this thing that I can read palm lines, and I never fail in it. I guess it runs in my family; my mom is a fortuneteller."

"That is interesting! What can you see in my future?"

"Have you been in any relationship before?"

"Once," I said, while you crossed my mind and rushed into my veins.

"It wasn't a serious one, was it?" she continued asking.
"What do you mean?"

"You knew or he knew it won't end up in marriage," she said, without looking up to me.

I swallowed my fear so she wouldn't notice and said "continue…"

"You're going to have one more relationship and it will be a strong, happy, long marriage." This time she raised her head and looked into my eyes with a soft smile, "You will get married at age 28."

"Really! That is a relief, not too early and not too late," I said. "I'm not excited for marriage anyway, there are things that're more important."

"Can you tell me more about the first relationship?" I asked with curiosity.

"I don't want to do this. I feel bad, and I don't want to tell you something that is bad. It is scary to know about your future."
"I didn't read mine because from looking at it, I don't like what I see," she said. "I don't want to know about my future,

I only want to know about this future, that it could be in the past one day."

My hand was still between hers, she looked down, and for the first time, I heard nothing but silence and my heartbeats racing. Why? Why was my heartbeat racing? What was there that I feared so much to know but I still insisted on knowing, and why did I believe her?

The palmists are liars even if they say the truth.

"There are two lines which join to become one but then split to be two again; the lines keep diverging away from each other, but there are branches coming from one of the lines to join the other, but the line never joins again and the branches end."

"The branches come from which line, mine or his?"

"Yours, these branches indicate some connection between you and him, you come to appear in his life from time to time and he never pushes you away, the branch line always joins with his line, but then it will stop, by you. You will stop coming back to him.

But his line isn't easy, he has or is going to have a busy life, maybe busy in work or busy going into many relationships."
"Could it be both, busy and relationships?" I asked.

"No, it is one of the two, mostly busy life. He isn't a man with one job. He is not like a teacher who teaches in school and gets back home and so on. No, he is a man with several jobs."
I stared at her and said, "Why, from all examples in the world, you said a teacher?"

She stared back, "I don't know, is he?"

"Yes!"

From a moment of ridicule to a moment of belief, she was right in every word she said, and I cared about nothing but his line.

"Can you tell how long it will take until my branches stop going to him?"

"Four to five years from now, but always remember the lines change with time, with your way of thinking and decisions you take. It's because you always have the choice, in these lines I can see that it's all in your hand."

I wasn't sure if her words were right or this was my eternal fate.

"Is he happy? Can you tell me if he is happy?" I asked with pain rushing into my heart.

"Dear, this line isn't his life. This line is his life with you only, and it ends with you ending with him. But I can only tell you, he is busy in life, maybe to overcome his unhappiness or maybe to be distracted from things that make him weak, make him feel lost. Probably his work is his life, his reason to be alive."

I looked at my palm, touched the lines, and somehow, I felt safe and happy for having part of your lifeline engraved on my palm, forever.

It's a faint line that's barely seen, but it's there forever. Like you, a whispered wind that crosses through my bones but overturns all my balances forever.

She also said I will have one serious relationship in my life; a strong, long and happy marriage. It's a beautiful, straight, deeply engraved line, unlike yours.

But you weren't just a dim relationship. You were more than destiny buried on my palm, you were darker.

I bet if she could read my heart, she would see an artery wrapping around it to keep its part together and she will point at it and say, "This is him, this is his line."

I went back home and I give it a second thought. The line is going on because of me, if I stop, the line will end. You won't fight back, you won't grab my line to keep it alive, you will not fight for me.

I had my coffee next to me. Lit a cigarette, took a deep breath. Held my breath to give it time so it goes deeper into my soul. Then exhaled slowly. Held the pencil, grabbed a paper and started to sketch. One hand inhaling smoke. The other hand exhaling my darkness on a scattered paper. Stopped, took a sip of coffee. Slowly, as if it's my last sip. Inhaling the cigarette as if it's my first inhale, and back to sketch our dark souls.

Together, side by side. It took me a while to draw those eyes. Black, sharp eyes, with a spice of sparkles, the sparkles I see when you look at me. Lit a new cigarette, inhaling deeper. Feeling the burns in my chest. The same chest you rested your head on, finding your way home.

I sketch you, to memorize your features. I sketch you and wonder if it is really you.

Hear me out! I'm living in my own chaotic world and it shows in my beauty. I was in unknown chaos and you came to show me the known one, the one that you brought with you. There is beauty in it, even in my hardest times. I bloom in the dark. Shall not fear your darkness. I survive and because I love you, I will save you too. If my light is fading in your darkness then

I will make sure to be your best darkest side and still will save you, will save both of us.

Close your eyes and go to where your heart tells you. It's not the light that you need. It's the darkness within you that will guide you to where you belong, and you belong with me.

This is the power of our love, accepting you as you are and not willing to change you. Not willing to take you any darker or any lighter. But I will show you what you never saw, feel what you never felt, and touch what you never knew. And this is all in me. Then you have the right to choose, and if your choice is away from me, then so be it.

Because I love you, and my love is not willing to change you. So I sketch you, making sure not to change anything in you.

But I've changed through the years, through our journey. My light fades away. My soul wanders into the dark. My heart is on the edge of despair. And my mind, my mind is in a conflicted state. How could I save you if I can't save myself? Is that even possible? Are we even in need to be saved?

Halfway, I stop sketching myself, where am I ending? I can't even recognize the soul my body is carrying. But I recognize yours well, I've been focusing on you for so long that I neglect mine. And here comes the time I realize "as long as we are together we will surpass everything" is nonsense speech because there was never any togetherness, there was only me

against everything else.

Chaos

Lost in His World.

Despite all the clashes between us, I found chaos in your darkness and you found serenity in my lighter side.

*Every time you leave me
Somehow, in a way,
I see you coming back
It is like you left a piece of you with me
A precious piece
And without it
You're not able to move on. What wrong have I done?*

***

*Sweetheart, it wasn't your fault, no it wasn't.
It was mine; I brought you into this even though I knew the truth.
I was supposed to turn my back to you, to get myself back up,
but I lost my way back home.
I lost my way to where I was and found a new home, in you.
You were my missing piece.*

*And because she was fooled by many
She ignored the only truthful person
That crossed her soul.*

When you decide on something,
Keep your heart away.
It is better to have a right decision by the mind, feel the pain for days, months or years, rather than take a wrong decision by your heart and regret for the rest of your life! But she couldn't do that, her heart didn't allow it.
It was the wrong decision but she never regretted it.
He was her favourite mistake.

How you were and how I was.
And how each one of us was on different sides of the world.
And how fate planned to bring us together.
To forget who we were before we met.

I had been taught in dental school,
If the patient is not cooperating,
Whatever you do, and whatever advice you give, the patient will never listen because in simple words, he doesn't care and that is the worst patient you could ever have. Apply that to everyone and everything. If the person you love so much and care so much about doesn't care about you and what you say or do, no matter how hard you try, how hard you want to keep him safe and happy, it will all go with the wind because, again, in simple words…
He doesn't care.

When you set a fire and leave, it burns, it does not turn off on its own. It keeps on burning everything down to death and turn into ashes. And you set me afire many times and left me to burn all alone while you were watching. Oh boy, I didn't need space. I didn't need time to calm down. I didn't need a clear mind to act. I needed you! I needed you to turn the fire off.

"I want to go away to keep you on the right track,
Because I love you.
And being with me is losing life,
See how desperate you are when you're with me.
You are not the same happy girl I knew,
Your heavenly smile is fading away,"
He said.

Lonesome man is not the one who lost his beloved ones, but the one who lost himself. A man who lost his soul and mind in the darkness, walked among the crowd invisibly. But she believed in him and he found himself in her smiles. He could hear his heartbeats in her heart.

I left the place behind, left our memories there and locked the door.
To begin a new journey in a place far away, where the past can't find me.
But it is ironic how I see you every night in my dreams.
To wake up the next day with a memory and a feeling that you were beside me, lying in bed the night before, breathing my breath, living through my veins.

It's ironic how I sense your soul in my words.
When I write, it feels like our memories are engraved in a preserved tablet.
Sometimes I feel words will bring you back. Will guide you to the light.
To me.
Thus, I will keep writing. Write about us. To keep you alive.
Alive in my memories.

You believe that when you reach a certain level in your life, you will be happy. As if your work and gaining money is the guide to happiness and being busy all the time is the right thing to do, but you're missing the beauty of life. The love of your woman. The laugh of your children and their daily stories. You think that when you reach "there," you will be satisfied.
But when you're "there," be "here." You will ask for more until you reach a point you're not satisfied, you're not appreciating. You will never feel the gratitude. You will forget to breathe.

You did change my life.
You showed up for a reason.
And this reason was to save a man from the darkness. You saved me. Your smile did. Your soul brought the good in me and your purity defeated my demons. You, my woman, have shielded me from chaos.

I lose track; I do so each time you let go of my hand. It's exhaustive, pulls all the power in my soul and leaves me empty. Empty lost soul. It takes time to build up myself. Sometimes, it stays empty; sometimes, I forget the feeling of being so full, full of love, full of happiness, full of madness, full of safety, full of life. Sometimes, I remember how I used to be alive, and it's not a good thing to remember, to remember the beauty of my soul that I lost.

I find myself through you, I understand what I wrote when I see you understand it too. I know how I feel when I see your response. My soul is full when you live within it. Even though I can live without you, I still want to see you one more time, and when I do, I will still want to see you another last time, and so on. Only to fulfil my lost soul.

The very person who fulfils my soul had nearly destroyed me. I lose track, and every time I do, my only leader in this chaotic world, my world, is your dark shadow, which nearly takes me to nowhere, a maze.

When your love is true and honest, it's hard to walk away even though you know he doesn't deserve it, but your pure love always tells you "give it a chance," and when you finally decide to walk away, love will hold you back and you will keep trying, doing all your best to work it out. Although deep in your soul, you know it will end soon and when it does, it will be with a broken heart, your own heart.

Then when it happens, and you finally let it go, you will pretend to be strong at day and fragile at night, in the dark your soul mourns. You act as if you never loved him, in fact, you will say it out loud, "I never hated anyone as I hated him," but your heart will never heal.

Don't be ashamed of your pain, of your weakness, embrace it. Speak up and let it all go with the wind. When you do, your heart will breathe again, ready for a new, true love. But this time, the true love could be self-love, spiritual love or forgiving love. Whatever kind of love, as long as it's a true one, it will heal your heart.

So let's pretend it's worth all the pain. Let's hope we will get out of this with no regrets. Let's believe that our soul will not be traumatized by our choices. Let me know that you're worth it all and that the feelings I felt were real and you are real.

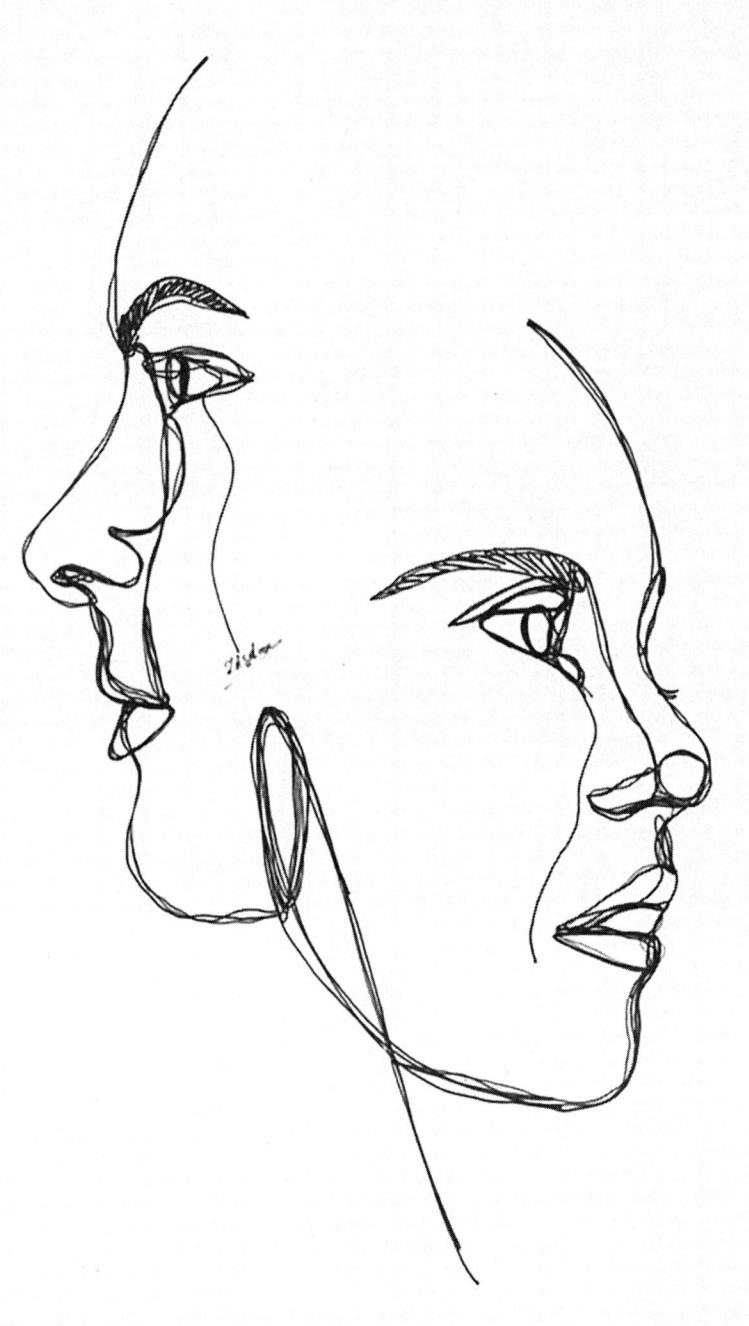

Sacrifice

I Cannot Blame You, You Loved Him.

He took her love for granted, because he knew, no matter how far he goes, she would still love him.
Love him with anger.
But she never understood this, or maybe she didn't want to open her eyes because truth hurts.
She chose her comfort zone, believing that it's better than the unknown.

You know why we change through time?
Someone enters your life and becomes a part of it, part of your everyday, but eventually their journey in your life ends and it is time for them to leave, when they do, they take a piece of you and leave it with a gaping hole. With time, these holes will take over your soul and you will never be the same person again.

They say when the heart speaks up, the mind must shut up.
Is that what she went through?
And what kind of heart is that to withstand all the pain and lies in the name of love?
Is that what love have become? Heartbreaker?

There are always stories about how amazing it is to fall in love but never about how it's so damn hard to fall out of love.

Pictures and memories scattered all over the place.
Good and bad days just passed like the speed of light.
People came and left. Enemies increased.
Nothing was right anymore.
Don't expect much in life.
And definitely don't expect much from someone who has nothing left.

*"You are perfect, believe it
You are!
And I'm so lucky
To have this perfection
In my life,"
He said.*

She is full of anger, hate and madness.
She is mad that he showed up in her life, angry because she knows he exists.
And she hates loving him.
She hates how deep he is in her soul.
And she is tired, tired from doing things against her will.
Tired of trying to walk away.
He wants to destroy her imaginative mind and make her like him, realistic and cold.

For a while, she trusted him and became as he wanted.
She thought realistic minds never got hurt.
But she wasn't alive.
She couldn't bear it.
She missed her world, her imagination.

You have the perfect balance of class and craziness.

You are beautiful
You're the law of gravity
You attract everything with a simple act
You are the centre of the earth
All the roads lead to you.

She knows he is not a beast
He is only human
And humans make mistakes
She also knows, no, she believes
That he is a good man
But not when she is next to him
And the only way to prove it
The only way to keep him safe
Is to walk away.

Even if no one else does
I will still pray for you to always be safe.
Forcing myself to fear you, to distrust you, to hate you in order to ask you to leave.
This was the only way.
I crumbled in that chair next to you like a child feeling cold.
You extended your arm in order to hold my hand, taking my fear away and supplied me with warmth.
But I distanced myself because I knew, once we have an encounter, I will collapse and grasp you tighter into this life.

***

I know you were surprised. You thought I fear you, the truth is, I fear myself, from getting weaker and more attached to you.
Why did you show up?
Why did you make me love you that much?
You knew the truth, you will never be mine!
You had your own life, your own little family.
Why did you love me when you knew this love had to end?

"I never thought it would end like this. For me it was just a few talks, breaking the routine, becoming friends, maybe. But with time, I got trapped in my little lie. And this game turned against me. I loved you, I still love you. I know it has no end. I tried to walk away, remember? But you didn't allow me, you always had a way to keep me in your life, to bring the peace and light back into my soul. I couldn't break your heart and leave you."

But we were never together. I was your daylight, and your family was your night.
I wanted you for all day and for the rest of our lives.
It's not greed, it is love, pure love.

I couldn't let you go after you told me the truth. You asked me to hate you.
I never hated anyone; I haven't hated those who hurt me, those who never touched my heart.
How could I hate the one I truly loved, the one who conquered my heart?
Three years I thought this love will end, we worked so hard to end this love but we're not good at stopping our love for each other, are we?

"Stop being emotional, be realistic. You knew the truth from the start and you decided to stay, and you held me into you more and more. This love had no future and you knew this. You decided to continue so you must bear the consequence. I have no time for love and your emotional moments, I'm a busy man and my career is more important than anyone."

I loved you. My heart felt like it didn't belong to me anymore, didn't fit in my chest. I couldn't control it, it was yours and I didn't want anything in return, just your heart was enough, and you failed to give me that.
Truth is, you don't know what love is, this only happens through the purity of the heart and the peace of the mind.
Your eyes were so dark. The place suddenly got cold. Fear ran through my veins.
You were a stranger.

There is nothing to say to a stranger.

I ran in a street full of cars and creatures but I felt lonely and lost. I headed to the shore and wondered at the waves, how they flounder against each other and turn upside down then interweave together in one place within the sea, while far from my sight, the sea appeared clear and calm.
This is how we are. Different feelings struggle at a point of loss and despair in one soul, one body, while others see in us peace of mind and a smiley exterior.
Don't judge a book by its cover.
How did we come to this? Perhaps the truth will set us free. Perhaps the truth was never you and me.

Regret

If I'd known I'd say goodbye to you,
I wouldn't have said hello in the first place.
I wouldn't have…

You know things get easier. With time it gets easier. The more you practice it, the more you go through it over and over again, it gets easier. First time is always the hardest, but then it gets easier. You fall in love easily. You end a relationship simply. You get hurt and heal easily. You start all over again in no time. You know what you want and get what you want easily. You say yes easily and no with no hesitation. Life treats you hard and you accept it. You stop fighting for a better life. The moment you realize things get easier is the moment you know you can't change people's attitude. The many times you fall and find no one to lend you a hand. It gets easier. It gets easier to be alone, to survive. It gets easier to accept disappointment from others. It gets easier to know the lies from the truth. Everything gets easier with time because everything becomes numb to you.

***

"I'm sorry for what I have done. Never thought it might hurt you that much, my love. You are my treasure and will always be. I thought if I told you this, you will walk away and I will stop the pain I caused you. I never meant to hurt you. Forget the pain I caused you. Forgive me for breaking my promises. Forget that day. You are my secret and will always be. And this is the beauty of our relationship,"
He said.

The more you delay doing the things you are supposed to do now, the more is the chance you will never do it.
And this happened with us. We agreed to walk away when it was the right time, when the fact of walking away immediately was the right thing to do, but time was never on our side.
Time made it difficult to move on. Time proved to us that somehow we would be connected.
Connected by the soul of love.

It can change one's belief, it can destroy someone's happiness. It can inspire you and drive your mind to a different life. It can raise you high or pull you to the bottom. It can cause war or create peace.
A word, if it was a lie or the truth, it changes everything.
As one word made me forget who I was when we met. One word ended everything between us. Ended what never existed. Because your word made it worthless.

"Soon, baby," he said.
Her heart skipped, her breath got shallower. And she waited, planning for that day. Dreaming how it would be.
Feeling his arms around her waist.
Thinking what she will say.
And she kept waiting.
But his soon wasn't as she thought.
His soon never meant soon!

At a certain point, I felt weak, weak when you were away and weaker when you were too close.
I felt so weak that I forgot how strong I was. But as I said, that was at a certain point. I realised that these weaknesses, when they gather up, they either give you power or take away your soul.
It depends on how much you learned and in what way you want to end.
For me, these weaknesses gave me what I always wanted to have and your presence gave me the trigger; you gave me the cause, the aim and the power. You gave me the book.

Remember that till this moment and to my final breath, you're still in a special place, hidden and safe.
Remember that I'm in your past, I'm here now and I will be in your future.
Remember that you're good, because I once lived in your heart.
Remember this, remember me.

When she knew the truth, the truth about his identity, there was not much difference because she didn't love his name or his money, she didn't love what he owned. She loved him, she loved his soul, his heart.
She loved his laugh and his sparkling eyes, his shivery voice that only she can hear and that never changed.
But this night, she saw a different man, she couldn't recognise him.
This night she knew her man was gone.
And there was nothing to fight for.

Enough is enough!
She had enough from the pain he caused
Enough from the love he pretended to give
Enough from him
She had enough from herself
From the one he had moulded her into.

She stood and was about to look back,
Was about to turn back to him, but then she realised that the man behind her was a stranger.
That man had only his shadow but not his eyes, not his voice.
That man didn't have his soul, his heart.
At that moment, she knew he was gone, there was no reason to turn back.
At that moment, she found herself on the right track.

He made her cry on her birthday.
Same as she cried on the day of her birth, the only difference was…
Her tears this time were with a wrecked heart and disappointment and the only wish she had before blowing the candles was not to be heartbroken again, never feel the pain he had caused and stop falling deeply into his heart forever.

The last thing he gave to her
Was a touch
A word
A drop of tear
A wipe
And engraved memories.

He brought her laugh back after she lost it.
And he remembered the first time he heard her laugh. He said after a long silence,
"Keep it, keep laughing because it turns everything dead back to life."
And now when she laughs, she remembers him, she remembers, although she thought she forgot.

There is no good in goodbye
But in our case it is
Goodbye…

Acceptance

Imagination vs. Reality

"Don't forget us!"
"Never, what we had is bigger than anything, it's so special and only because of you it happened."
"Promise me, promise me, you will love me forever."
"I promise."
"Not this way, say it!"
"Okay! I promise I will love you forever."
This is how the story ends, like all stories, one day it will be forgotten. All that will remain is the trace of black ink on a piece of paper.
But I knew it was real, I knew he was real and I knew one day he will find a way back, a way through my words.
But this wasn't how it ended in reality; destiny had a different ending; a painful, strong one.
I never accepted his family, the reality of having a home full of kids and a wife next to him at night. These made me insane and develop uncomfortable thoughts which affected my actions towards him; it created a gap that neither of us liked. And because I'm not accepting his reality, I created my own imagination about us: the prefect picture of a happy couple, which of course didn't last long and the image collapsed as soon as his reality hit me back.
I remembered there was a time I admired his family so much because they were a part of him and I was willing to do anything for them, but when destiny let me meet one of his children, I learned that some doors are meant to be closed.
But I never opened up my concerns and my emotions because I didn't want to hear his silence and I couldn't blame him, he couldn't deny his only true thing, his reality, his family.

And so it came to the light of our relationship in forms of anger, trust issues, boredom, sadness, fear and disturbance. Love faded, never like our first time. And I didn't see it, didn't understand the cause of agitation between us. And he lost the admiration, the joy, the very first feeling he had for me; affection.
There was a time in my story when I cringed at the corner and cried, letting out all the pain, all the fear and all the anger to fulfil my emptiness with serenity, acceptance and love.
I stopped the tears, not because I no longer sensed the fear and weakness but because I had to leave that corner. I needed to gather my thoughts and stand up in one piece. So I stopped crying and I started to think what led me to that corner.
And I came up with this: I realised that what dragged my soul to the darkness, what shattered me, what led me to that cold dark corner, wasn't you, it was me!
And so taking action was needed, because our story can't end like this. I had to protect the legacy, the love, our memories. With baby steps, I began to accept that he is who he is because of his reality and that his family is a part of him and that can't be changed.
I realised that I no longer needed to change or fix him. I no longer needed to create our own life and that accepting him with his reality was the healthiest thing to do.
In fact, the problem was never in accepting his reality but in accepting my reality with him. It was a self-acceptance issue and so I made an agreement with myself to appreciate, validate, and support myself, despite deficiencies and negative past behaviour. I made peace with my soul.
I had this feeling that, despite the presence of stress, I could keep myself in a calm state, a state of acceptance of who I am and a milder and tentative form of happiness; it is satisfaction, and I would fight not to lose it in any way.
But then you gave me a hit, a strong one. You broke all the promises and all the trust. You showed me that it was a lie, everything was a lie. You ruined everything.

You destroyed us, the memories we built and the love I believed in so strongly, you shattered me. You killed the good and burned what I sowed.

And I realised that the only cause I'm fighting for, the only cause I'm protecting in creating more memories, is the thought that you actually loved me, but you didn't.

You made a home out of me and you promised to keep it away from chaos but you didn't.

I created so many memories without realising that someday they will cause so much pain.

And so I've changed…

I'm a grown-up person who no longer needs to smile at every photo. I no longer laugh at every joke. I no longer answer "I'm great" at every "how are you?" I no longer like caramel in every coffee drink. I no longer feel awkward eating alone in public.

I no longer need you in every failure and definitely not in every success. I no longer need to tell you how I feel about us to fix it. I no longer need your chest to feel safe. I no longer need to hear your voice to sleep. I no longer love winter because it reminds me of your warm body. I no longer feel alive because you have taken the best in me. I'm a grown-up person but I can't stop loving you.

Yet, I'm letting you go.

That's what grown-up people do!

I went from a raging, angry person to a calm, silent person. I walked away silently without facing you with the truth and asking you for an explanation because there was nothing to explain and because I knew you will burst out lies, assuring me you love me, but your actions spoke before your lips.

"Will you please talk to me, get your anger out, fight with me, act dramatic and tell me what bothers you, do what you always do when you are mad at me."

Why? It has been five years, one thousand eight hundred twenty-five days and each day had a special memory. I'm so tired of fighting for the sake of saving this love. I'm too exhausted and powerless to discuss with you and hear your lies. I'm full of pain. I couldn't look into your dark eyes and ask you to be honest with me. You gave me the worst feeling I could ever feel: disappointment. I'm disappointed that you proved everyone right and let me down. I held so many hopes on you, I was so damn proud of you. I would hold your hand and walk among the people, in the light, showing the world how much I'm proud of you.

I worked so hard to make you a human, a man with a heart, but you've always liked to be the devil.

You need to understand that things aren't the same. Cartoons are no longer my priority. Writing made things worse; it's not my salvation anymore. Remember my excitement over a baby bird walking the street or a child playing in the playground. It's gone. I stopped pretending to be afraid of heights to run between your arms. I stopped listening to people complain about life. I stopped the advices, the care and the love. I hate emotional talks. I hate deep discussions. I hate everything that reminds me of you. I've changed, like everyone else.

I love loneliness, the smell of black coffee with cigarette. I admire the dancing of the smoke coming out from between my lips. I didn't have any other desire but the desire for serenity and calmness. I sent my soul to the dark, swaying back and forth at the edge of loss and I didn't fear falling to the darkness. Because this time, my dark side isn't as yours, it's a cold, heartless side, built up by the pain you formed and the hate I developed.

I've been fooled for too long, holding on to feelings I never knew will turn out like this. Memories we created to carry on for the rest of my life, happy memories, but they turned to be painful ones.

At the time that I should have given up, I was creating more memories of feelings that would hurt me at the end. You said, "I won't hurt you. I will fix you." But I didn't need someone to fix me, I needed someone to embrace my pain. Said you won't leave me, but you also didn't plan to stay.

Even though I told you to let me go, I also wanted you to
stay and tell me you love me.
Isn't it painful when you love someone but don't get anything
in return? Maybe you loved me back but never showed it.
I never wanted to leave you.
But I needed to stop daydreaming, the mystery, the
endless hope of happily ever after.
I learned the hard way that you write the beginning of your
story but you can't end it the way you want it. I don't want
to get in trouble and I know you are the trouble, the one with
issues, not me. I was never at fault, even once.
I'm so exhausted, drained with a heavy, empty soul.
Filled with your darkness and my light is fading away.
I want to rebuild everything you destroyed, starting with
my heart.
So lie and tell me you love me for one last time, because
you are going to lose something you thought you will never lose.
I thought of taking revenge and I succeeded. I imagined it
will satisfy my pain and empower my pride, it didn't!
I fell into guilt, guilt of breaking your heart as you did
mine. My pain didn't heal, it became more painful.
My heart got broken twice, the first time was by you and
the second time was by me.
Ironically, my first revenge was for you, the very first
person I loved and whom I wouldn't dare to hurt in any way.
Guilt could be a curse to the soul same as revenge.
And my heart was heavy, I couldn't undo what I'd done,
but I could accept it, learn from it and move on for a better
soul and rightful heart.
I'd had enough of people coming into my life and leaving
with a piece of me.
Now I'm hollow and empty, there is nothing left for them
to take when they leave. I've got nothing to give and nothing
to worry about anymore.

And now that I've accepted reality and chosen serenity
and joy over anger and sadness, I can trust who I am again
and believe in my choices and never be weak again. There is
pain and hate and soon there will be regret in my choices and
with time, there will be an awakening from all of this.
And I will grow by my own. And I will bloom to give but
this time I will feed my soul. I will be selfish. I will be
generous to my heart. I will lock the door well, and let my
mind choose wisely.
And you will notice and you will try to come back, you
will be greedy. But I will be powerful enough to ignore and
armed well to protect my serenity and too wise to open the
door for you.

I am on the road of no return!

She fought for this relationship to end on good terms but it seems the universe fought back and won this time!

The door that brought storm, chaos and loss is the door you applied years of courage to close. Don't let one single fake memory reopen it.

The mind is the enemy here and imagination makes reality suck. We imagine the perfect love story, the first kiss, the greatest man. We keep imagining everything right and perfect and once reality hits, we get disappointed and never appreciate what we have.

But what if what we have is the perfection of reality?

Nothing should be called "being lost," it's only difficulty in reading your feelings. There are no lost places, only unknown places that need to be discovered by you.

Time to accept that some people are toxic, some places are painful and not all memories are blessings.
But I loved you.
And now I exhale you. I take out your chaotic world out of my home. You are no longer a weight on my chest. I'm lighter, giving back your world and setting my wings free. I let myself go. Searching for the other half that I lost with you, my other half, my light side.
Clear mind, lighter soul and new home.
A home away from your chaos.

Fight for what you love until you stop loving it.
And I stopped loving you.

You folded the page and moved on. I created a book about us and watched it burn to ashes.

I used to hear stories of broken-hearted people and get overwhelmed about them…until my heart got broken and ever since then, when I hear heart-breaking stories, I'd be like… Oh! You will live, grab a seat.

She had to fight him, block him, hate him and ask about him at his back.
She had to do what kids do when they are mad! Because she is not a grown-up person, not when she is in love!

It hits! And when it does, it strikes hard. Again and again. Because it's not stable. Not deep enough. So it hits with a slight memory, with a touch, with a familiar smell. Anything that reminds me of you! It hits the deepest, darkest moments and when it comes out to the light, I collapse. Not from weakness. I buried you in my darkest side, buried my emotions, the love I had for you, the memories. I buried them all along with myself to survive and move on. But at my darkest night, it hits! And I lose track, I lose the cold me. Why do I do that?

Because when I loved you, I gave it all and became full of emotions. And to unlove you, I gave it all again to be emotionless. I do that and become the person with no feelings and no living heart until it stops hitting back!

I don't know what will happen next, but I do know I will never give it all again!

The Theory of Everything

Dear Reader,

Everything has an end…keep it in mind and you will never get disappointed. Happiness ends with sadness and sadness ends with joy.
Love can end with hate and hate can end with love.
Everything has an end but they don't end the same way.
It can be a happy ending or a desperate ending or it can be a lesson.
It can end in any way…
It depends on your acceptance and satisfaction to that end.
So you fight for the end that you want and you never stop fighting because you believe, you have faith and you know your hard work will not go with the wind and you know if it ends in another way, at least you fought for it.
Victory and Defeat are immaterial; it is the fight that counts. And because you don't want to regret, you don't want to take the chance to think, "If I fought for it, I would have had it."
Because you, as a human, never give up and for this reason, God chose human among all the creatures to seed and build this planet because He knows you are capable of everything. He knows you are not easily defeated.
You don't run from fear, you run toward it to break it, to gain from it strength; like the darkness, you walk through it to find the light you don't fear because you believe.
You believe…

And I believe. I believe in fate. I believe in the power of choice and believe in you and what is within you and I have no fear.

Because I know from darkness, the light comes; and from weakness, the power comes; and from evil, the good comes; and from you, everything else comes; everything that matters to you most.

Everything in this life starts and ends with you. To win a war, you have to win the small fights. The first fight you should win is the fight of having your people in one line.

My people are the mind, heart and soul.

Having these three in one line makes me invincible.

Doing what is right, this is my mind; and doing it with love, this is my heart; and doing it to last forever so it transfers from generation to another, this is my soul.

They were never meant to work against each other.

They are in one body and meant to be together.

When you take a decision and your heart keeps pestering you that something isn't right, listen to your heart because your subconscious is speaking to you and that is something divine, and when you do, negotiate with your mind because this is a gift. God gave it only to us among all the other creatures. When they are both in one line, bring your soul in for the performance.

Fear doesn't keep you safe; it holds your talent back, drags your actual purpose in this world far away. Don't fear to lose, because losing is the beginning of winning. Don't fear to become weak because the feeling of weakness makes you eager to become stronger. Don't fear something that you have no clue about, don't fear the unknown.

I won't lie. I fear the upcoming, and we all do! The fear for the unknown is a very destructive feeling.

But here comes the power of faith; believing for the best from the future and having faith that everything happens for a reason makes us not fear anything.

So, don't kill the present just because you are thinking of the future.

Life is like a game. In each game there are levels, the game starts with an easy level and trains you to get ready for the upcoming levels which are harder.
And during the game, the founder of the game has provided you with some weapons: extra life, three lives and some hints.
Sometimes you need to pay extra money to get more supplements.
You keep going from level to level, sometimes you get stuck in a level a bit longer, repeating it, and every time you do, you learn a new trick or maybe notice things you missed before. It takes time until you pass the level and when you do, you yell out loud, "YES!" As indication that you made it with pride and you go to a new, harder level with confidence and excitement.
In real life, your life is the game and the founder that provides you with weapons and chances is you. Yes, you.
The fact of not giving up and trying over and over again is your weapon, the power of strength. Believe it's your weapon and there is always a chance to fix things and to learn from your mistakes. If God gave you chances and forgiveness, you too can provide that and have mercy on your soul.
It's okay sometimes to pause your game and rest, to reduce the tension and relieve your stress, to gain confidence and think how to pass the level.
But there are times you will be out of chances, out of strength. There are times you will be empty in soul and lost. You will need to buy new supplements. The money that you use in the games to get new supplements, in real life I call it praying.
Pray to God for mercy. Pray for guidance. Pray for help; ask for a hint if your choice is right or wrong.

See it in this way and I assure you, your mind, heart and soul will be in one line.

Remember, you are the founder here, you're the one who provides the entire weapon you need and you're the one who

decides whether to stop or continue. And herein comes my previous statement,
Everything starts and ends with you.

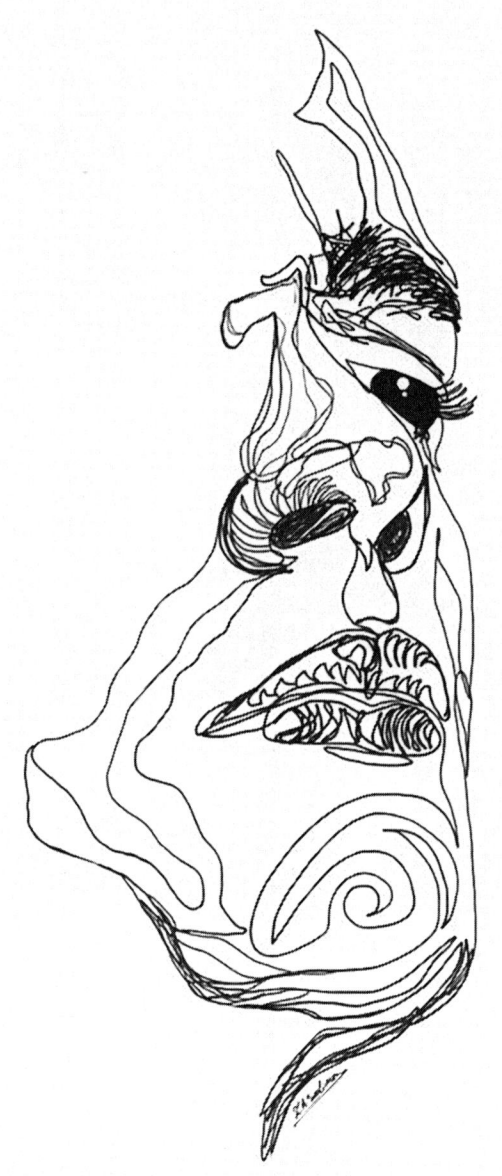

Beloved memory,

I've loved and I've lost and between the two, gained a lifetime of wisdom.
The eye doesn't see what the brain doesn't know. I had no clue who you were except what you told me. Whether lies or truth, my feelings were sincere.
The eye doesn't see what the brain doesn't know, and the heart holds onto what will not break it to parts.
But I had doubts, doubts in your stories, doubts about your identity. I had doubts that you're too perfect to exist but your simple words, "Please don't worry about your doubts, listen to your heart," only pumped the heart and encouraged it to take a step to its favourite mistake.
The eye doesn't see what the brain doesn't know. I wasn't blind, I wasn't immature or irresponsible. I was just unaware of the consequences of my choice, because I didn't see the truth behind or maybe I neglected all the facts, thus, I didn't see where I was going.
I had no map to direct me because I was clueless where I was heading and trusting you happened to be the only map I had. I followed my instinct and your shadow which made me reach here, between the lines of my own words.
It guided me to this, our story; our feelings filled the scattered pages to create the most memorable feelings, to form this; the book.

Note this, that after each goodbye, I held my hopes high, hoping to see you one day as we always did after any goodbye.

So I held my hopes high based on this. Based on what we went through, based on being lovers forever. Then I thought, "Meanwhile let me try to let you go too, maybe it will work this time. After all, this is how it should be."
So I stopped talking to you in my mind every day, I stopped seeing you in the dark side. I made myself busier all day and night.
But I couldn't stop you from passing by in my dreams or hearing your name in my name.
Until the day came, the day I thought will never come, because you never told me you could be a liar. I couldn't breathe and I couldn't speak either.
And I knew this time it was real, I fainted, and my hopes fainted with me.
How could you do that?
You had me without any experience and you left me with experiences.
The experience of falling in love and being loved.
The fear of losing.
You gave me experience of how the mind and heart can work separately and become stubborn against each other. You taught me that listening to the heart only and neglecting the mind could turn your life upside down.
You taught me to be realistic and that emotion makes me weak, the same emotions that I loved you with.
You made me see how love can fade away and how I can lose it and this is the worst experience.
Hating, cheating, manipulating and breaking hearts were the only things that you failed to teach me.
And I'm glad you failed.
But I can understand how you managed to let me go.
Something like erasing that time from your life, as if I never existed, but this was never true!
You never shut a door against me.

Let me tell you how I will manage to move on.

I was fragile and weak, took my strength from you,
believing that our love is enough and as long we are together,
we will pass everything.
But now I can observe a different situation and trust my
instincts to lead me to the right direction, a pathway away
from you. To search for my own desire and search life for serenity!
Deep down I must have known that you weren't my
journey. But I was so scared of leaving my comfort zone and
discover life without you. I was afraid of the unknown.
But now I accept our reality and I don't fear the future
because whatever the future will be, it will not be based on lies.
The new road must be rough and challenging, but I trust I
can conquer it all.
I have my way in everything, especially in letting go.
You flipped the page, and I created a book to remind me
not to go for that mistake again, loving you.
I don't regret what I did as much as I regret what I didn't do!
With no regret, you were my favourite mistake.
But life will never stop me, you—will never stop me and
will never stop anyone else. I have to set myself free from the
prison of memories.
It is time to stop wasting my energy on others who are not
willing to pay me back. So I will move on but without erasing
that time from my life.
To remind myself what I've learned and not to give all of
me to others, although all of me was gone to you!
There are not enough words to say what you are to me.
You will always be in a special place in my heart.
A beautiful memory, a friend, a companion, a dark side
and once a lover because you see, my friend, a heart that once
felt what love is will never fill its heart with black venom of
hate; and those who live with hate will never be happy in life,
will never forgive and forget and will never know the feeling
of love.
Hate is heavy.

It consumes you from inside; we think it's a weapon to attack those who harmed us.

However, hatred is a double-edged weapon, and the harm we do to others, we do to ourselves too.

This powerful hate won't get me anywhere, but the charm of forgiveness which arises due to true love will lead me to a positive life.

It's okay. I don't know how to hate and you don't know how to love.

Time can never mend.

Time only eats your soul slowly until you lose yourself and there is no comfort in the truth. Pain is all you will find, till you accept it.

The truth is we don't need time to heal, we need time to understand why it happened. Because everything becomes easy when you understand it. Everything becomes normal when it's not odd anymore. And there is plenty of time to understand, accept and embrace all the chaos and misunderstanding.

Then there will be no pain.

So it is me who should mend all this because I'm born to love, to be happy, and dragging myself into depression for so long is nothing but weakness and I was never weak; I never gave up on the bright side.

I can be whoever I want whenever I want, and no creature can stop me from that. This memory will always give me strength to move on.

To find my aim and pure soul…

My friend, my love, my choice, my lesson, my favourite mistake, my divine.

Thank you!

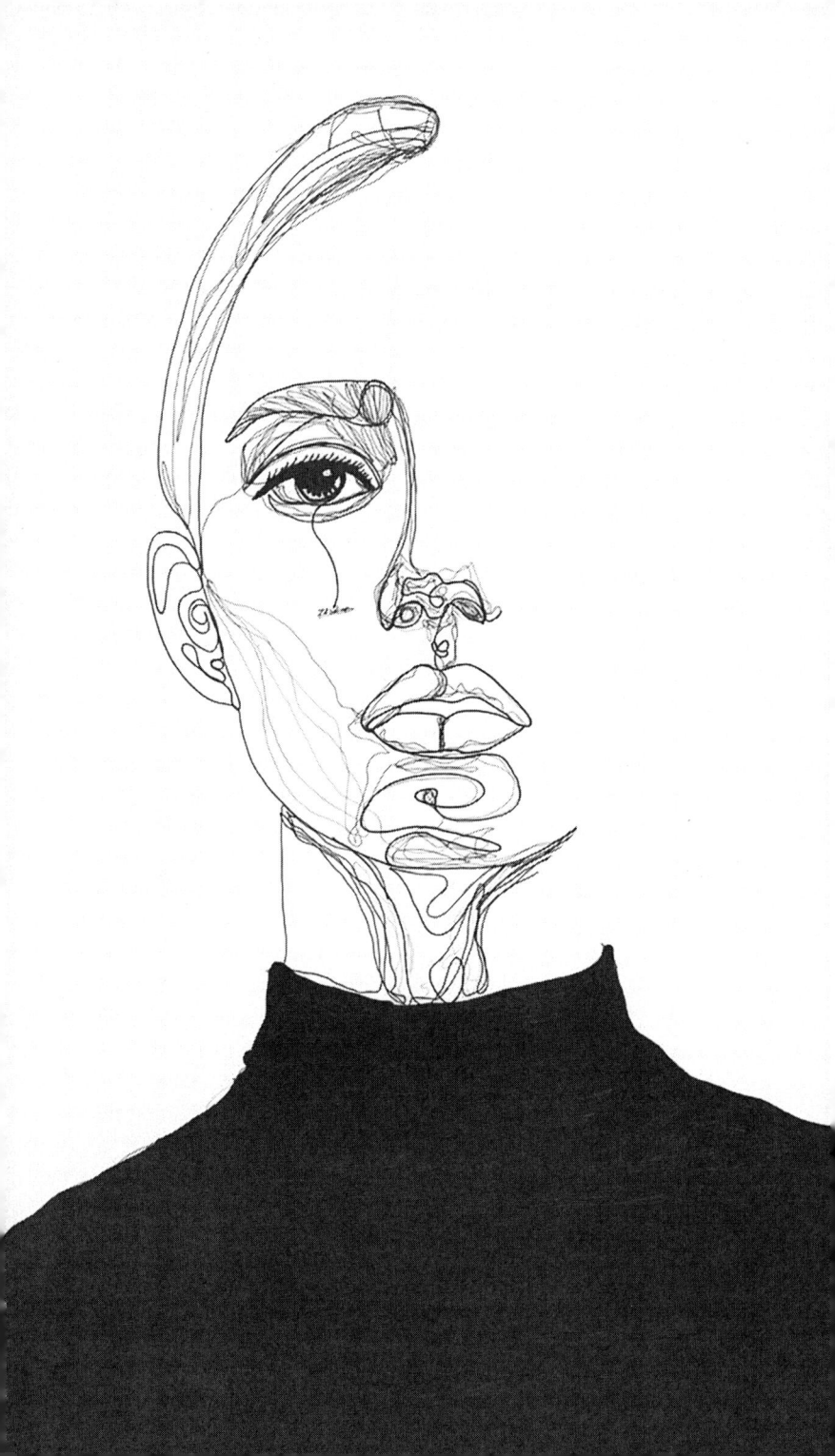